A Story of Three Trees

ISBN 978-1-64028-366-4 (Paperback)
ISBN 978-1-64114-069-0 (Hard Cover)
ISBN 978-1-64028-367-1 (Digital)

Christian Faith Publishing, Inc.
296 Chestnut Street
Meadville, PA 16335
www.christianfaithpublishing.com

Printed in the United States of America

A Story of Three Trees

ARIANA DELGADO

What you are about to read is the story of the three trees,
Who stood together in the meadow, swaying in the breeze.
Each one was different in purpose, splendor, and might,
But each was equally important in God's kingdom and God's sight.

Every story has an order and every story has a flow,
But this story has a secret, and I think that you should know.
This story starts at the end and is going in reverse,
Moving toward the beginning, word by word and verse by verse.

Part of the story that is mentioned is about the three trees,
Who are but a representation both of you and of me,
And how individually their lives had unfolded,
Living out God's purpose for which they were molded.

The other part is about Jesus and all that he has done,
About how he's our savior and God's only son.
And how he changed people's lives wherever he went,
Bringing hope and salvation as you will see in each segment.

Our story begins with a tree named Cedar,
Who wanted to grow up to be a great leader.
He wanted to be the tallest, this was his ambition,
But what we find is that this didn't ever come to fruition.

But Cedar wasn't really one who was considered vain,
He just wanted to know his purpose, it was driving him insane.
What he desired more than anything deep down in his heart,
Was to use his height to point to God and always do his part.

Cedar was unappreciated, not held in high esteem,
To him being overlooked had become a common theme.
He was told he was not special, only worthy of the scrap pile,
But God looked past his shortcomings and made him feel worthwhile.

They cut Cedar down and stored him away,
Where he was then forgotten, much to his dismay.
But during this time he never lost hope,
And turned to his faith, which helped him to cope.

At some point in his future much later on,
Cedar was remembered one day after dawn.
He who was forgotten, ridiculed, and pushed aside,
Now found himself where his dreams and his purpose would collide.

For now in this moment Cedar realized that he was picked,
And everything in his life that led to this moment just clicked.
Because where he started as a tree, he was fashioned into a cross,
And the moment he was chosen for left him at a loss.

Now Cedar was being carried and slowly pulled along,
By the man named Jesus as he was beaten by the throng.
Wrongfully accused and condemned to death,
Cedar was there for Jesus's last breath.

Cedar's ultimate goal of pointing to the Lord,
Became a reality and became his reward.
What happened that day will never be diminished,
It was Jesus who proclaimed that it is finally finished.

Next in our story we have the mighty oak tree,
With his mighty oak branches and his mighty oak leaves.
He was big, he was strong, and what he wanted the most,
Was to be turned into a ship that would cause all to boast.

He wanted to carry royalty, he wanted to win wars,
One of his ambitions was to conquer foreign shores.
Those who cut him down were well aware of his great strength,
They saw his great circumference and were awed by his great length.

But the turn of events in Oak's life were rather unexpected,
And where he ended up left him feeling quite dejected.
Oak did not become an imposing military force,
And this was a hard hit that knocked him off of his high horse.

Oak was taken and was carved into just a simple boat,
Made for nothing more than keeping a few fishermen afloat.
One day he was boarded by a small group of thirteen,
And the challenge that lay ahead of them still remained unseen.

There was a storm that day at sea, unexpected and severe,
It made twelve of Oak's passengers cry out desperately in fear.
The waves just kept on coming, the storm would not desist,
Yet one passenger was sleeping as if the rain was just a mist.

13

The twelve passengers woke Jesus, they were afraid that they would drown,
They were scared because they felt that the whole boat was going down.
But Jesus posed a question as the boat was rocked and swayed,
He looked directly at them and asked, "Why are you afraid?"

When Jesus spoke to the waves, how quickly everything did cease,
And the twelve disciples were then overwhelmed with peace.
Oak witnessed such a miracle upon the water that day,
Which made him realize that he could no longer downplay

That he did indeed carry the greatest royal to exist,
And he was chosen for this time, for this purpose: to assist.
When Oak thought his life was nothing and it did not go as planned,
In the end he came to the conclusion that God's ways are always grand.

So when you're overwhelmed by the waves of chaos and of strife,
Never forget that you can follow the way, the truth, and the life.
The words of Jesus always tell us what is real and what is true,
And if you choose to listen, there is nothing you can't get through.

The final tree in our story was beautiful and fine,
She was regal and majestic, and her name was Pine.
She wanted to be adorned with diamonds and with gold,
She wanted to be a sight for everyone to behold.

Pine was resilient and remained evergreen,
All year she was fresh, and she sat like a queen.
The woodcutters not only acknowledged that she was pleasing to the eye,
But everyone would delight in her sweet fragrance as they walked by.

Above all, Pine dreamed of carrying great treasure,
Possessions so rich in value that no man could measure.
And when her time came to be cut to the ground,
In no way was she happy about what she found.

She was made into nothing more than a manger for food,
She was plain and would get soiled as the animals chewed.
Forever condemned to a life among beasts,
Not among riches or fancy parties and feasts.

She was not taken to a palace far, far away,
She was placed in a barn and surrounded by hay.
This reality hurt Pine, her ego did it sting,
But she had no idea what her future would soon bring.

There was a young family who was seeking a place to sleep,
Little did they know that they'd also be staying with the sheep.
For because of the census, all the rooms in town were full,
But the innkeeper still had some strings that he could pull.

He placed them in his barn and put a roof over their heads,
It was all that he could offer because he ran out of beds.

Mary was loved by God and very highly favored,
But the task that God gave her was not initially savored.
She was told by an angel that she was going to conceive,
But she was a virgin, so she found that hard to believe.

The angel then continued and said she would soon give birth,
To a child named Jesus, who would bring salvation to the earth.
He would be the Son of the Most High who would reign forever,
But now it was up to Mary if she would undertake this endeavor.

She was obedient to the Lord, and she chose to have her son,
Because in her life she only wanted to see God's will to be done.
Unknowingly, she and Joseph went to where the star did shine,
To the place where they would eventually come in contact with Pine.

This is the point that they could all begin to see God's hand,
For this was the greatest miracle to happen throughout the land.
The baby was born and placed in the manger,
And there is nothing that can be considered any stranger,

Than knowing that this little baby was king,
And that because of his birth every angel did sing,
And yet here he was being cradled by Pine,
In a humble manger that most would decline.

But this moment was special, this moment was rare,
This moment was one that was worthy of prayer.
Because in this moment Pine finally understood,
That God didn't forsake her and that His plans are good.

Pine's dream came true, and she held the most precious treasure,
So priceless that it brought her heart nothing but pleasure.
She was aware that this baby would soon grow up,
And that the purpose was extraordinary for which he showed up.

To take our transgressions, our sins, and our mess,
And turn it into something that would eternally bless.
Because of this baby, Satan is forever defeated,
And every last one of God's promises is completed.

This concludes our story of the three trees,
Whose lives were not always filled with comfort and ease.
At times there was disappointment, and struggle, and grief,
But they were always in God's hands, down to their last leaf.

Things didn't turn out the way that they thought,
But they received greater blessings than they had originally sought,
Because God has a way of turning things around,
Even when our dreams are shot to the ground.

Each one was made into something that was not their first choice,
But each one was given more than they asked for, and they rejoiced.
As a cross, Cedar is now symbolic of Christ,
Who for our sins was sent and was also sacrificed.

Oak was not turned into the type of vessel one would think,
But his life is a reminder that God will never let you sink.
As a manger, Pine has shown us that God is never far,
And what you look like doesn't matter, what matters is who you are.

Each one of us can do things we have never even dreamed,
Because each and every one of us has a chance to be redeemed.
God has offered us a gift that each one can receive,
But it is up to you to consider what it is that you believe.

About the Author

Ariana Delgado was born and raised in Northern Virginia, where she still resides. She has a bachelor's degree in psychology from Marymount University. She is working toward becoming a chaplain by seeking a master of divinity degree with a chaplaincy concentration from Liberty University. This is her first publication.

Lightning Source UK Ltd.
Milton Keynes UK
UKHW051913121022
410367UK00004B/71